KU-214-540

# ISSUES today

# Crime in the UK

**Edited by Christina Hughes**

Vol.111

Series Editor: Cara Acred

**Independence Educational Publishers**

# Acknowledgements

The publisher is grateful for permission to reproduce the material in this book. While every care has been taken to trace and acknowledge copyright, the publisher tenders its apology for any accidental infringement or where copyright has proved untraceable. The publisher would be pleased to come to a suitable arrangement in any such case with the rightful owner.

Illustrations

All illustrations, including the front cover, are by Don Hatcher.

Images

All images courtesy of iStock, except page 4 © Pennywise, page 20 © Pixabay and page 24 © Kashfi Halford.

Editorial by Christina Hughes and layout by Jackie Staines, on behalf of Independence Educational Publishers.

Printed in Great Britain by Zenith Print Group.

Cara Acred

Cambridge

May 2016

# Contents

## About *ISSUES* today

**ISSUES today** is a series of resource books on contemporary social issues, designed for Key Stage 3 pupils and above. This series is also suitable for Scottish P7, S1 and S2 students.

Each volume contains information from a variety of sources, including government reports and statistics, newspaper and magazine articles, surveys and polls, academic research and literature from charities and lobby groups. The information has been tailored to an 11 to 14 age group; it has been rewritten and presented in a simple, straightforward and accessible format.

In addition, each **ISSUES today** title features handy tasks and assignments based on the information contained in the book, for use in class, for homework or as a revision aid.

**ISSUES today** can be used as a learning resource in a variety of Key Stage 3 subjects, including English, Science, History, Geography, PSHE, Citizenship, Sex and Relationships Education and Religious Education.

## About this book

*Crime in the UK* is Volume 111 in the **ISSUES today** series.

The prison system as a whole has been overcrowded in every year since 1994. This book looks at different types of crime – which are going up and which are falling – as well as those suffering in silence, young lives behind bars and children's experiences of visiting their parents in prison. It also addresses crime prevention methods such as forecasting crime hotspots, the increase in armed police and questions the use of the death penalty.

*Crime in the UK* offers a useful overview of the many issues involved in this topic. However, at the end of each article is a URL for the relevant organisation's website, which can be visited by pupils who want to carry out further research.

Because the information in this book is gathered from a number of different sources, pupils should think about the origin of the text and critically evaluate the information that is presented. Does the source have a particular bias or agenda? Are you being presented with facts or opinions? Do you agree with the writer?

At the end of each chapter there are two pages of activities relating to the articles and issues raised in that chapter. The 'Brainstorm' questions can be done as a group or individually after reading the articles. This should prompt some ideas and lead on to further activities. Some suggestions for such activities are given under the headings 'Oral', 'Moral dilemmas', 'Research', 'Written' and 'Design' that follow the 'Brainstorm' questions.

For more information about **ISSUES today** and its sister series, **ISSUES** (for pupils aged 14 to 18), please visit the Independence website.

# Crime in England and Wales

## Year ending March 2015.

➤ Latest figures from the Crime Survey for England and Wales (CSEW) showed that, for the offences it covers, there were an estimated 6.8 million incidents of crime against households and resident adults (aged 16 and over). This is a 7% decrease compared with the previous year's survey, and the lowest estimate since the CSEW began in 1981.

➤ The decrease in all CSEW crime was driven by a reduction in the all theft offences category (down 8%). Within this group there were falls in the sub-categories of theft from the person (down 21%) and other theft of personal property (down 22%). However, there was no significant change in other sub-categories such as domestic burglary and vehicle-related theft.

➤ In contrast to the CSEW, there was a 3% increase in police recorded crime compared with the previous year, with 3.8 million offences recorded in the year ending March 2015.

➤ The rise in the police figures was driven by increases in violence against the person offences (up by 23% compared with the previous year). However, this increase is thought to reflect changes in recording practices rather than a rise in violent crime. The CSEW estimate for violent crime showed no change compared with the previous year's survey, following decreases over the past four years.

➤ Offences involving knives and sharp instruments increased by 2% in the year ending March 2015. This small rise masked more significant changes at offence level with an increase in assaults (up 13%, from 11,911 to 13,488) and a decrease in robberies (down 14%, from 11,927 to 10,270). In addition, the related category of weapon possession offences also rose by 10% (from 9,050 to 9,951). Such serious offences are not thought to be prone to changes in recording practice.

➤ Sexual offences recorded by the police rose by 37% with the numbers of rapes (29,265) and other sexual offences (58,954) being at the highest level since the introduction of the National Crime Recording Standard in 2002/03. As well as improvements in recording, this is also thought to reflect a greater willingness of victims to come forward to report such crimes. In contrast, the latest estimate from the CSEW showed no significant change in the proportion of adults aged 16–59 who reported being a victim of a sexual assault (including attempted assaults) in the last year (1.7%).

➤ While other acquisitive crimes recorded by the police continued to decline there was an increase in the volume of fraud offences recorded by Action Fraud (up 9%) largely driven by increases in non-investment fraud (up 15%) – a category which includes frauds related to online shopping and computer software services. This is the first time a year-on-year comparison can be made on a like-for-like basis. It is difficult to know whether this means actual levels of fraud rose or simply that a greater proportion of victims reported to Action Fraud. However, other sources also show year-on-year increases, including data supplied to the National Fraud Investigation Bureau from industry sources (up 17%).

*16 July 2015*

**www.ons.gov.uk**

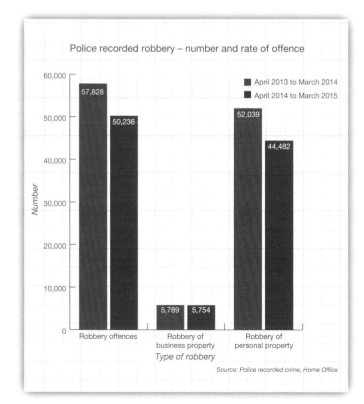

Police recorded robbery – number and rate of offence

- April 2013 to March 2014
- April 2014 to March 2015

*Number*

60,000
57,828
50,236
52,039
50,000
44,482
40,000
30,000
20,000
10,000
5,789  5,754
0

Robbery offences | Robbery of business property | Robbery of personal property

*Type of robbery*

Source: Police recorded crime, Home Office

## Mini glossary

**Acquisitive crime** – *a crime committed to gain possessions. This includes the following crimes: domestic burglary, theft of a motor vehicle, theft from a motor vehicle and robbery (people and business).*

# Which crimes are going up and which are falling?

Why are some crimes in the region falling, while others are on the rise? David Powles investigates.

The year is 2003 and Norfolk Police is being swamped by vehicle-related crime.

In the 12 months previously their figures show they dealt with 11,440 such offences.

That is about one-sixth of all recorded crime in the county, hours of manpower and lots of pain and disruption for the victims.

Fast-forward 11 years and that figure reads very differently.

While overall crime has fallen, vehicle-related offences have gone down – there were 2,334 in the whole of 2014. It is the same in Suffolk, where vehicle crime fell from 7,152 to 3,186.

This is just one area where, according to the statistics, certain crimes are being driven out of our communities.

Yet our study of recorded police statistics for the past 11 years show this is not the case for all offences. In Norfolk, Suffolk and Cambridgeshire, shoplifting, drug offences and violence have bucked the trend.

Crime experts question whether the statistics can be trusted.

There are two main ways crime is assessed in Britain – using figures provided by police forces and the Crime Survey for England and Wales.

There have been concerns about the reliability of those issued by forces and last year the UK Statistics Authority withdrew their gold standard status after hearing evidence of forces under-recording.

Dr Nic Groombridge, criminologist from St Mary's University at Twickenham, believed they could still be a useful tool to track emerging trends.

He said: "There is a vast amount of crime that isn't picked up by police records, the crime survey or other organisations. Some crimes aren't reported, sometimes people don't even know they've been a victim of crime.

"But these figures are a good indication of the reasons people have for calling the police."

So why have some risen, while others fall?

As far as vehicle crime is concerned technology has played a big part.

Dr Groombridge said: "This is one we can be fairly confident about. The reduction is largely down to car

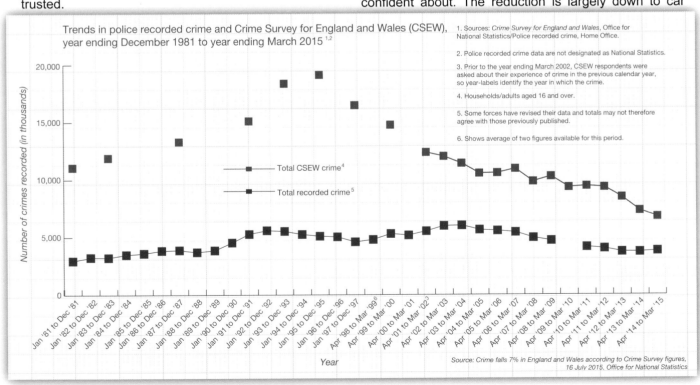

Trends in police recorded crime and Crime Survey for England and Wales (CSEW), year ending December 1981 to year ending March 2015 [1,2]

1. Sources: *Crime Survey for England and Wales*, Office for National Statistics/Police recorded crime, Home Office.

2. Police recorded crime data are not designated as National Statistics.

3. Prior to the year ending March 2002, CSEW respondents were asked about their experience of crime in the previous calendar year, so year-labels identify the year in which the crime.

4. Households/adults aged 16 and over.

5. Some forces have revised their data and totals may not therefore agree with those previously published.

6. Shows average of two figures available for this period.

Source: *Crime falls 7% in England and Wales according to Crime Survey figures, 16 July 2015*, Office for National Statistics

manufacturers suddenly realising that security was a factor as to why people brought cars and improving security measures."

The same can be said for burglary and cycle theft. There were 3,820 house burglaries in Norfolk in 2003, compared to 1,311 last year. In Suffolk they fell from 2,284 to 1,391.

Even though cycling has become increasingly popular in recent years, crime prevention has improved and the figures have remained relatively static.

Elsewhere, theft in Norfolk fell from 11,987 to 5,781 and Suffolk from 6,224 to 4,794 and robbery from 579 to 199 in Norfolk and 249 to 164 in Suffolk. The picture was similar in Cambridgeshire.

Experts said crime was moving behind closed doors.

Dr Groombridge added: "There is a school of thought that people who were previously out on the streets offending, committing burglaries and robberies, are now back at home doing it in the cyber world on games such as *Grand Theft Auto*.

"But what we are seeing is an increase in cyber offences. We've moved towards a cashless society which makes one type of crime less likely, but opens a new door."

And what of those crimes that are on the rise? In 12 years, shoplifting in Norfolk has risen slightly from 3,730 to 3,857, but there was a sharp spike in 2007, 2009 and 2011. In Essex the figures rose from 3,289 to 3,663.

That was when the recession hit hard and people were more likely to take desperate measures.

Violence offences, with or without injury, rose slightly in all counties, while there was also a rise in sex offences from 729 to 1,300 in Norfolk and 634 in 2003 to 1,028 in Suffolk.

Dr Groombridge said: "Generally police will say these figures have risen because reporting has gone up."

Historic sex offences have featured heavily in the public eye in recent years and this will have impacted the figures.

Norfolk Police also dealt with many more drugs offences in 2014, rising from 1,392 to 2,579, while Suffolk drug offences also rose, but Dr Groombridge claimed this may be a case of police putting more priority on to it.

In general, official crime has fallen dramatically for all three of our forces, and Dr Groombridge said: "I'm fairly confident that crime is going down. I suspect, however, that a lot of people will think that crime is not going down as there is always a problem of perception."

# What now for crime?

Many experts in criminology share the view that cyber-related crime will become more common place.

One reason for this, according to Dr Groombridge, is because many of these crimes currently go unreported. Eventually the statistics will catch up with the true picture.

Meanwhile, as anti-crime technology improves, this will have an impact. Dr Groombridge said: "In terms of shoplifting we are still waiting for technology to catch up. When they put tracking devices on items such as bottles of whisky or clothes it prevented people from stealing them. But the smaller items don't currently have them. There may come a time when they will.

"The reason mobiles are so popular to steal is that they are mobile. They can be taken, then used. There will come a time when technology makes it harder to make use of a stolen mobile."

Dr Groombridge believes there is a danger that technology can take things too far.

He explained: "There is an enormous amount we can do to drive down crime completely if you are really hell-bent, but would we want to live in a society like that?

"One of the downsides of freedom is you have to have some crime.

"I am concerned by the things we have done in terms of some of the smaller crimes, those police previously may have turned a blind eye to.

"If everything is monitored on speed cameras and CCTV you are going to get more crimes and going to need more jails. At a low level we are seeing lots of things criminalised to some level, e.g. fines for parking.

"If you say you want to completely eradicate crime you have to be careful as you may lose a lot of freedom as well."

*11 May 2015*

www.edp24.co.uk

# Buying and carrying knives: the law

The laws about buying and carrying a knife depend on the type of knife, your age and your circumstances.

## Basic laws on knives

It is illegal to:

- sell a knife of any kind to anyone under 18 years old (16- to 18-year-olds in Scotland can buy cutlery and kitchen knives)
- carry a knife in public without good reason – unless it's a knife with a folding blade three inches long (7.62 cm) or less, e.g. a Swiss Army knife
- carry, buy or sell any type of banned knife
- use any knife in a threatening way (even a legal knife, such as a Swiss Army knife).

Lock knives (knives with blades that can be locked when unfolded) are not folding knives, and are illegal to carry in public without good reason.

**The maximum penalty for an adult carrying a knife is four years in prison and a fine of £5,000.**

## Good reasons for carrying a knife

Examples of good reasons to carry a knife in public can include:

- taking knives you use at work to and from work
- taking knives to a gallery or museum to be exhibited
- the knife is going to be used for theatre, film, television, historical re-enactment or religious purposes, e.g. the kirpan some Sikhs carry.

A court will decide if you've got a good reason to carry a knife if you're charged with carrying it illegally.

## Banned knives

There is a ban on the sale of some knives:

- flick knives (also called 'switchblades' or 'automatic knives') – where the blade is hidden inside the handle and shoots out when a button is pressed
- butterfly knives – where the blade is hidden inside a handle that splits in two around it, like wings; the handles swing around the blade to open or close it
- disguised knives, e.g. where the blade is hidden inside a belt buckle or fake mobile phone
- gravity knives
- sword-sticks
- samurai swords (with some exceptions, including antiques and swords made to traditional methods before 1954)
- hand or foot-claws
- push daggers
- hollow kubotan (cylinder-shaped keychain) holding spikes
- shuriken (also known as 'death stars' or 'throwing stars')
- kusari-gama (sickle attached to a rope, cord or wire)
- kyoketsu-shoge (hook-knife attached to a rope, cord or wire)
- kusari (weight attached to a rope, cord or wire).

This is not a complete list of banned knives. Contact your local police to check if a knife is illegal.

*22 January 2015*

**www.gov.uk**

# Suffering in silence

Children and unreported crime.

## Executive summary

This report presents the findings of a Scoping Inquiry into the hidden victimisation of children and young people. The research was undertaken on behalf of the All Party Parliamentary Group (APPG) for Victims and Witnesses of Crime. The inquiry was in response to findings from the most recent Crime Survey for England and Wales which found that less than one-fifth of children and young people who experience theft or violent crime report this to the police. The charity Victim Support undertook research for the Inquiry in partnership with the University of Bedfordshire. Evidence was gathered in four ways:

> a short review of existing literature;
> an analysis of relevant data sources including the Crime Survey for England and Wales;
> a rapid call for evidence from charities, service providers, statutory bodies and campaigners; and
> three focus groups with children and young people.

## Findings

### 1. Children and young people experience much higher rates of crime than police data suggests

> Research shows significant levels of crime and victimisation amongst children and young people. Approximately one-third of 11–17-year-olds, for example, report experiencing physical violence within the last year. One-quarter of 11–24-year-olds say they experienced some form of abuse or neglect during childhood.
> Evidence shows that children and young people are at higher risk than adults of experiencing certain forms of crime. For example, females aged 16 to 19 years are the age group at highest risk of being a victim of a sexual offence.
> Existing vulnerabilities, such as a long-standing illness or disability, appear to really increase children and young people's vulnerability to crime.

The majority of crimes against children and young people are not reported to the police. Only 13% of violent offences and 15% of thefts are reported by young victims. Similarly, only 5–13% of adults who were victims of childhood sexual abuse reported it at the time.

### 2. Children and young people don't always know what can be considered a crime and how to report this

> Many children and young people do not realise that what they have experienced is a crime. This is particularly true where forms of criminal behaviour are seen as normal within a friend group or a community.
> Children and young people don't always know how to report experiences of victimisation. Teachers are the professionals they are most likely to tell but they, and other professionals, often lack confidence about how to recognise and respond to reports of children's victimisation.

### 3. The situation in which the crime happens affects how likely the victim will report it

> The fact that much of children and young people's victimisation occurs in settings, such as school, where offenders are known to the victim reduces the possibility of a victim choosing to report crime.

### 4. Children and young people fear what might happen to them if they report a crime

> Children and young people were worried about the risks of reporting a crime, such as damage to their reputation, what might happen to their family or fears of physical harm.

> Unwritten group 'rules' in certain social circles encouraged others not to report crimes to authority figures. There was also a fear of the offender threatening or blackmailing the child or young person to keep silent.

## 5. Children and young people may blame themselves for being a victim

> Many children and young people falsely assume the crime was their fault. Where children and young people feel in any way responsible for being a victim they are unlikely to report these experiences or seek support.

## 6. Negative views of the police means children and young people are less likely to report a crime

> Many children and young people have little confidence that the criminal justice system will deliver justice and protect victims.
> Children and young people's attitudes towards the police are often due to feelings of mistrust and fear. Many believe that the police treat them more negatively than they do adults and feel that the police will treat them with a lack of respect, suspicion or discriminate against them.

## Case study

Even where children and young people had a sense that what was happening to them wasn't right and they wanted to report this, evidence from the focus groups found that there was a lack of knowledge about the most appropriate way to do this. Several young people said they were uncertain on how to report incidents where they weren't in immediate danger and didn't feel a 999 call was necessary:

"From what I've seen young people are fairly confident regarding bigger crimes. If it's someone's house gets broken into, that's definitely a thing for the police whereas if it's like bullying and cyber bullying, it's generally approached as the sort of thing that's dealt with by like schools or heads of year and maybe people aren't quite sure how the police would go about that." (female, group 3).

"You need better education about what actually happens when you report a crime…they tell us these numbers – like 999 and 101 – but they don't tell us actually what happens when you call one of those numbers. What do you have to say? What should you expect?" (female, group 2).

*9 December 2014*

**www.victimsupport.org.uk**

### Mini glossary

**Blackmail** – *the use of threats to force someone to do something. This threat could be violence or the threat to reveal some information about a person they would rather be kept private.*

**Victimisation** – *when someone is treated badly.*

# Young victims of crime: understanding the support you should get

If you're a victim of crime, support and information is available to help you get through it.

The Victims' Code is a Government document that tells you what support and information victims of crime in England and Wales should get from criminal justice agencies. These are organisations like the police and the courts. The Victims' Code has a special section for people who are under 18 because they should get extra support.

## Telling the police about the crime

You can tell the police about a crime by phone, online or by going to the police station. The police should give you information so you know what happens after you've told them about the crime and what support you should get next.

Unless you say you don't want this, the police will give your contact details to a charity that gives help to victims. Someone from the charity will get in touch with you to offer their help or support.

You can have an adult stay with you while the police ask you questions about what happened. This could be your parent or family friend, but they need to be over 18 years old.

You may be asked to make something called a witness statement. This is when you say what happened when the crime took place, like what time it was and where you were. The police will ask you if you also want to make a Victim Personal Statement (VPS). This is when you say how the crime has made you feel and how it has changed things for you. The VPS lets you tell the judge and others in the court room how you feel about what happened to you.

You don't have to make a VPS if you don't want to, but if you do choose to make one, it can be made at any time before the case goes to court. Once you have made a VPS and signed it, you can't take it back or change it but you can write another one to give more information to the police and courts.

You will be asked if you would like to read your VPS out in court if the suspect is found guilty. You do not have to do this if you don't want to and can ask for somebody else to read it out for you instead. If you don't want your VPS to be read out in court at all, the court will still look at it before they decide what punishment to give to the suspect.

## Knowing what's happening

The police should get in touch with you or your parents to let you know how they are looking into the crime and whether anyone has been arrested or charged for the crime.

You can tell the police how often you want to hear from them about the investigation and how you would like to be contacted.

## Going to court

If your case does not go to court, you should be told why not. If there is a trial, you may be asked to be a witness in court, this means you will have to speak in court to tell them what happened.

If you are a witness at court, you should be told about what this means for you and should be kept up to date with information with what's happening. This includes:

➢ information about where and when the court hearings will take place

➢ whether the suspect has been allowed to go home until the court date or is being held in prison.

Also:

➢ you may able to visit the court before the day of the trial if you want

➢ someone from the Witness Care Unit should contact you before you go to court to answer all your questions about going to court and to help you until the case is finished.

## After the trial

If you've been a victim of a sexual or violent crime, and the suspect is sent to prison for more than 12 months, you will be able to join the Victim Contact Scheme. Victims on this scheme can get updates on what happens to the suspect after they go to prison and can give their thoughts on any rules the suspect must follow when they come out of prison. If you are under 18, your parent or guardian can decide to use this service to get updates and to pass on your views.

## Being a witness

If you go to court as a young witness in a trial you may be able to use 'special measures' to help make it easier for you to tell the court about the crime. Special measures are things like:

> having a screen around the witness box so that you don't have to see the suspect or their family when you are answering questions

> being able to give evidence by live video-link so you don't have to be in the same room as where the trial is taking place

> the judge and lawyers remove their wigs and gowns to make you more comfortable

> having someone, called an intermediary, be with you in court to help you understand the questions you are being asked.

You can also ask people who work at the court if you can wait in an area away from the suspect and their friends and family.

## Restorative justice

As a victim you may be able to take part in restorative justice. This is when you have contact with the offender so that both of you can find a way forward and build a more positive future. It gives you a chance to tell them how the crime has affected you so they can understand the impact of their crime. The offender is also able to say why they did the crime and say sorry if they want to. Both you and the offender need to agree to this before it happens. You do not have to take part in Restorative Justice but you will be given lots of support if you decide to write to or meet the offender.

## Gary

### Gary, 15, attended a restorative justice meeting with the offender who had mugged him:

"At first it felt strange to be so close to the offender. The officer who was there was a big help. Each person had a chance to speak. My family and I talked about how we were affected and so did the guy who mugged me. As he explained what happened and why – basically it was down to drugs, drugs, drugs – our anger went away. We all signed an agreement at the end, which included suggestions and changes that would improve the life of the offender and (hopefully) stop him committing more crimes in future.

"I am glad we attended the conference. The great thing about it was that the offender got to hear what it was like for me and was very sorry. We too got to see into his life and understood better what had driven him to crime."

*The above information is reprinted with kind permission from The Ministry of Justice. © Crown copyright 2016*

**www.gov.uk**

# Prison: the facts

Bromley Briefings Autumn 2015.

## Key facts

➢ On 23 October 2015, the prison population in England and Wales was 85,106.[1] Between 1993 and 2014 the prison population in England and Wales increased by more than 40,000 people, a 91% rise.[2]

➢ Prison has a poor record for reducing reoffending – 45% of adults are reconvicted within one year of release. For those serving sentences of less than 12 months this increases to 58%.

➢ Over two-thirds (68%) of under 18-year-olds are reconvicted within a year of release.[3]

➢ Reoffending by all recent ex-prisoners costs the economy between £9.5 and £13 billion a year.[4]

➢ Short prison sentences are less effective than community sentences at reducing reoffending. People serving prison sentences of less than 12 months had a higher reoffending rate than similar offenders serving a community sentence – they also committed more crimes.[5]

➢ Prisons are getting bigger. 45% of prisoners are now held in prisons of 1,000 places or more.[6]

➢ There are now fewer staff looking after more prisoners. The number of staff employed in the public prison estate has fallen by 30% in the last five years – 13,730 fewer staff looking after nearly 1,200 more people.[7]

➢ Serious assaults in prison have risen by over a third (35%) in the last year.[8]

➢ More children are affected by their parents being in prison than divorce in the family.[9] Around 200,000 children in England and Wales had a parent in prison at some point in 2009.[10]

➢ Looked after children make up 33% of boys and 61% of girls in custody,[11] despite fewer than 1% of all children in England being in care.[12]

## Prison sentences

➢ Prison sentences are getting longer. The average prison sentence is now nearly more than four months longer than 20 years ago by 15.9 months.[13]

➢ Increasing numbers of people in prison don't know if, or when, they might be released. Indeterminate sentences account for 18% of the sentenced prison population, up from 9% in 1993.[14]

## Children and young adults

➢ The number of children (under-18s) in custody has fallen by two-thirds in the last seven years.[15] They are also committing fewer crimes – with proven offences down by 72% from their peak in 2005–06.[16]

➢ At the end of March 2015 there were 1,004 children in custody in England and Wales. 44 children were aged 14 or younger.[17]

1    Ministry of Justice (2015) Population and Capacity briefing for Friday 23 October 2015, London: Ministry of Justice

2    Table A1.2, Ministry of Justice (2014) Offender management statistics prison population 2014, London: Ministry of Justice and Table 1.1, Ministry of Justice (2015) Offender management statistics quarterly: July to September 2014, London: Ministry of Justice

3    Tables 16a, 17a and 16b, Ministry of Justice (2015) Proven reoffending statistics: July 2012 to June 2013, London: Ministry of Justice

4    National Audit Office (2010) Managing offenders on short custodial sentences, London: The Stationery Office

5    Ministry of Justice (2013) 2013 Compendium of re-offending statistics and analysis, London: Ministry of Justice

6    Ibid

7    Table 2, Ministry of Justice (2015) National Offender Management Service workforce statistics bulletin: June 2015, London: Ministry of Justice and Table A1.1, Ministry of Justice (2015) Offender management statistics, Prison population 2015, London: Ministry of Justice

8    Ibid

9    Office for National Statistics (2011) Divorces in England and Wales 2009, Fareham: Office for National Statistics

10   Ministry of Justice (2012) Prisoners' childhood and family backgrounds, London: Ministry of Justice

11   Kennedy, E. (2013) Children and Young People in Custody 2012–13, London: HM Inspectorate of Prisons and Youth Justice Board

12   Department for Education (2013) Children looked after in England year ending 31 March 2013, London: DfE, StatsWales website, and Office for National Statistics (2013) Population estimates total persons for England and Wales and regions Mid-1971 to Mid-2012, London: ONS

13   Table Q5.1b, Ministry of Justice (2015) Criminal justice statistics quarterly March 2015, London: Ministry of Justice and Table 2.3, Home Office (2007) Sentencing Statistics 2005, London: Home Office

14   Table A1.1, Ministry of Justice (2014) Offender management statistics prison population 2014, London: Ministry of Justice and Ministry of Justice (2013) Story of the prison population: 1993 - 2012 England and Wales, London: Ministry of Justice

15   Table 2.1, Youth Justice Board (2015) Monthly youth custody report - March 2015, London: Ministry of Justice

16   Table 4.2, Ministry of Justice (2015) Youth Justice Statistics 2013- 14 England and Wales, London: Ministry of Justice

17   Table 2.1 and 2.8, Youth Justice Board (2015) Monthly youth custody report - March 2015, London: Ministry of Justice

- Children spend an average of seven months in custody, including time on remand.[18]

- One in five children in custody surveyed reported that they had learning difficulties.[19]

- Assault rates amongst children in custody are rising. In 2013–14 there were 15 assaults per 100 children in custody, up from 9 in 2009–10.[20]

- Fewer than 1% of all children in England are in care,[21] but looked after children make up 33% of boys and 61% of girls in custody.[22]

- The minimum age that a person can be prosecuted in a criminal trial in England, Wales and Northern Ireland is ten years. This compares to 12 years in Canada, 13 years in France, 14 years in Germany and China and 15 years in Sweden. In Scotland the age of criminal responsibility is eight years, but the minimum age for prosecution is 12.[23]

## Mothers and fathers

- During their time at school an estimated 7% of children experience their father's imprisonment.[24]

- It is estimated that more than 17,240 children were separated from their mother in 2010 by imprisonment.[25]

- Only 9% of children whose mothers are in prison are cared for by their fathers in their mothers' absence.[26]

- Parental imprisonment approximately trebles the risk for antisocial or delinquent behaviour by their children.[27]

- Over half (54%) of prisoners interviewed had children under the age of 18 when they entered prison. The vast majority felt they had let their family down (82%).[28]

- 40% of prisoners said that support from their family, and 36% said that seeing their children, would help them stop reoffending in the future.[29]

- Women are often held further away from their families, making visiting difficult and expensive. The average distance is 60 miles, but many are held considerably further away.[30]

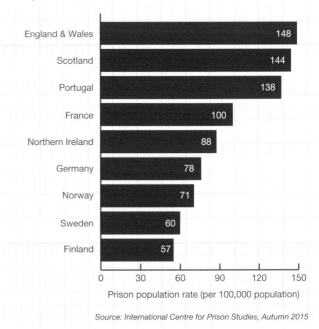

## Imprisonment rates across Western Europe

| Country | Prison population rate (per 100,000 population) |
|---|---|
| England & Wales | 148 |
| Scotland | 144 |
| Portugal | 138 |
| France | 100 |
| Northern Ireland | 88 |
| Germany | 78 |
| Norway | 71 |
| Sweden | 60 |
| Finland | 57 |

*Source: International Centre for Prison Studies, Autumn 2015*

18  Table A3.1c, Ministry of Justice (2014) Offender management statistics annual tables 2013, London: Ministry of Justice

19  Gyateng, T., et al. (2013) Young People and the Secure Estate: Needs and Interventions, London: Youth Justice Board

20  Ibid

21  Department for Education (2013) Children looked after in England year ending 31 March 2013, London: DfE, StatsWales website, and Office for National Statistics (2013) Population estimates total persons for England and Wales and regions Mid-1971 to Mid-2012, London: ONS

22  Kennedy, E. (2013) Children and Young People in Custody 2012–13, London: HM Inspectorate of Prisons and Youth Justice Board

23  Jacobson, J. and Talbot, J. (2009) Vulnerable Defendants in the Criminal Courts: a review of provision for adults and children, London: Prison Reform Trust; and http://www.scotland.gov.uk/ News/Releases/2009/03/27140804

24  Ministry of Justice (2012) Prisoners' childhood and family backgrounds, London: Ministry of Justice

25  Wilks-Wiffen, S. (2011) Voice of a Child, London: Howard League for Penal Reform

26  Baroness Corston (2007) A Review of Women with Particular Vulnerabilities in the Criminal Justice System, London: Home Office

27  Murray, J., & Farrington, D. P. (2008) 'The effects of parental imprisonment on children'. In M. Tonry (Ed.), Crime and justice: A review of research (Vol. 37, pp. 133-206). Chicago: University of Chicago Press

28  Ministry of Justice (2012) Prisoners' childhood and family backgrounds, London: Ministry of Justice

29  Ibid

30  Women in Prison (2013) State of the estate - Women in Prison's report on the women's custodial estate 2011-12, London: Women in Prison

# Young lives behind bars

## About the report

Children and young people who offend are among the most vulnerable and disadvantaged members of our society.

Yet despite their high level of need, children in custody are all too often overlooked or let down by health and social care services.

**"Children and young people who offend are among the most vulnerable and disadvantaged members of our society."**

To read the report in full please visit: http://www.bma.org.uk/working-for-change/improving-and-protecting-health/healthcare-for-vulnerable-groups/young-lives-behind-bars

## Sara's story: the journey into detention

### Age ten

When Sara was ten she was forced to leave the family home with her mother and sister because of domestic violence. Sara found the change difficult. She missed her father, at one point returning to live with him, but she had to leave when he again became violent.

By the time she was 13 she was struggling at school, she was truanting, mixing with older men, drinking and taking drugs. Social services eventually took her into local authority care although she ran away and stayed with friends. She had also started to harm herself, sometimes quite badly.

**"When Sara was ten she was forced to leave the family home with her mother and sister because of domestic violence."**

Her mother tried repeatedly to get Sara a referral to mental health services and she was eventually given a short voluntary placement in a psychiatric hospital to safeguard her. Sara improved and was discharged with the promise of an intensive support package.

Unfortunately the support did not materialise and Sara returned to her abusive and risky behaviour.

**"Despite the recommendation that she be placed in a therapeutic residential placement, Sara was given an extended sentence of three years in custody."**

Following conviction for grievous bodily harm, Sara spent nine months on remand before a forensic psychiatric assessment was finally funded. The assessment concluded that due to her age, Sara's problems were not yet clear cut enough to meet the criteria of the Mental Health Act.

Despite the recommendation that she be placed in a therapeutic residential placement, Sara was given an extended sentence of three years in custody.

MARRIAGE
FUTURE CAREER
FUTURE
PROSPECTS
FAMILY
LIFE

the view that Sara was not vulnerable but just 'badly behaved' and had brought the assault on herself because she had been drinking. No new offences had been committed but Sara was taken back into custody.

> **"Sara was unable to build on the educational progress made in custody because she was refused access to local colleges due to her history of violence."**

Sara's custody worker felt that, among other services, Sara needed additional child and adolescent mental health service (CAMHS) input. The secure unit had itself struggled to commission a service from CAMHS, although this changed during Sara's second return to custody when they took on a specialist CAMHS worker for the first time.

## Sara's story: the revolving door – in and out of detention

### Age 17

Sara struggled in the secure training centre (STC). She refused to leave her cell for the first six weeks and was eventually moved to a smaller 15-bed female unit. After establishing a close relationship with the youth offending team (YOT) worker she improved, managing her anger better and she began to reflect on her future.

Sara was released on parole at the age of 17 but was recalled following an angry outburst at one of the YOT staff. She spent a further nine months in the same small unit and again made good progress. She was released into supported accommodation and was offered 25 hours intensive support a week from the YOT.

She was also promised the support of a child care social worker (because of her period spent in care) to help her look for independent accommodation. Again, little of the promised support materialised. In addition, Sara was unable to build on the educational progress made in custody because she was refused access to local colleges due to her history of violence.

After six weeks back home, Sara got drunk with an older male who then assaulted her. The YOT took

## Sara's story: beyond detention, beyond childhood

### Age 18

With her 18th birthday approaching, Sara faced a number of further potential setbacks, including the departure of her trusted YOT worker from the smaller unit and a move to an adult female unit within the same prison. Just before her move, having not self-harmed for years, Sara tried to take her own life.

She didn't know why but said that everything had suddenly got on top of her. She was then assessed by a CAMHS psychiatrist and a mental health diagnosis was indicated for the first time.

Sara had by this time spent two and a half years in custody, and was likely to remain there for some time.

*2014*

**www.bma.org.uk**

# Locked out

Children's experiences of visiting a parent in prison.

*By Dr Jane Evans*

## Executive summary

This report is about children's experiences of visiting a parent in prison. The Government estimates that about 200,000 children are affected by parental imprisonment each year in England and Wales,[1] and each week, children make nearly 10,000 visits to public prisons.[2]

Outcomes tend to be worse for prisoners' children than for their peers. Yet they are hidden, because no one counts them, and stigmatised, because their families often feel ashamed to ask for help. Barnardo's, along with other voluntary organisations, supports prisoners' children both in the community and inside prisons.

We spoke to children at our community services, at prison visitor centres (where families wait before visits) and at prison visit halls. They told us what they experienced during prison visits, what worried them and what they appreciated.

The children and parents we spoke to are asking for small changes to the system, not major policy changes. They simply want their families' lives to be easier and to gain more from the relationship that they have with the parent in prison.

Some prisons, for example HMP Parc in South Wales, approach family visits as a valuable resource in the resettlement of offenders. They view visits as a family intervention, rather than a security risk or a privilege that can be given/taken away. Barnardo's encourages this. As well as improving outcomes for offenders and benefiting the prison, it is more positive for children.

### Article 9 of the United Nations Convention on the Rights of the Child

Children whose parents do not live together have the right to stay in contact with both parents unless this might hurt the child.

More children are separated from a parent by imprisonment than there are children in care. Thousands of visits to prison are made by children every year.

## Recommendations

Based on our research, we are making the following recommendations:

### 1. All prisons should view visits as a family intervention, rather than a security risk.

At HMP Parc, where visits are delivered as a family intervention rather than a security function, behaviour within the visits facility has improved, and there is greater engagement in family opportunities. There has been an impact on positive resettlement and rehabilitation. In addition, behaviour in the prison has improved and passing of contraband in the visits hall has declined.

### 2. Searches of children and babies should be made more child-friendly.

Prison governors should take a child-centred approach when it comes to security measures to help support the emotional wellbeing of children[3].

### 3. Children's visits to male prisons should be separate to the Incentives and Earned Privileges scheme, as they are for women's prisons.

The Incentives and Earned Privileges scheme gives out the length, frequency and quality of visits to prisoners according to their behaviour. This sharply impacts on visits that can be made by their children. Visit entitlements should be separate from the Incentives and Earned Privileges scheme, as they are in the women's prisons. In particular, family visit days should not be restricted to 'enhanced' prisoners. Children have a right to contact with their parents, including in circumstances where they are separated from a parent through imprisonment.

### 4. The National Offender Management Service should make applying to the Assisted Prison Visits scheme easier.

The Assisted Prison Visits scheme helps towards the cost of visits. However, it takes too long to find out about

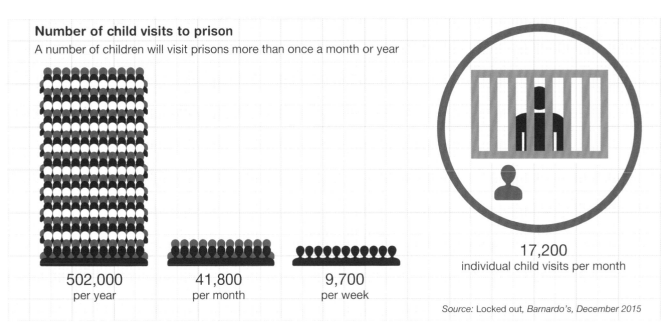

**Number of child visits to prison**

A number of children will visit prisons more than once a month or year

502,000
per year

41,800
per month

9,700
per week

17,200
individual child visits per month

*Source: Locked out, Barnardo's, December 2015*

the scheme and applying for it is too complicated, which causes hardship. With plans to build new prisons out of towns, this will become even more important as distances travelled for visits increase. Children with a parent in prison are at greater risk of child poverty[4] than their peers. The financial burden of visiting should not be a barrier to children enjoying their right to contact with their parent.

## 5. Play facilities and visitor services within prisons should reach a consistent national standard.

There is a lot of variation between prisons in terms of what is provided for children. While many excellent organisations provide play and support facilities in prisons, too many play areas are only for very young children, are often unsupervised or are even locked. Visiting a parent in prison should be made as positive an experience as possible, in order to support family relationships and children's wellbeing.

## 6. Children should be permitted to bring homework and school reading books into and out of prisons.

This is allowed in some, but not all, prisons. Governors should make arrangements to allow children to share their educational progress with parents in prison. This offers an opportunity to link into education for prisoners, many of whom have very low levels of literacy and numeracy. Prisoners may be motivated to improve their skills so that they are able to help their children with their schoolwork. Engaging parents in prison in family learning opportunities will help to mitigate the increased risks of poor educational outcomes for the children of prisoners.

## Footnotes

1. www.gov.uk/government/uploads/system/ uploads/attachment_data/file/278837/prisoners-childhoodfamily-backgrounds.pdf

2. Freedom of Information request (2014). Barnardo's, Barkingside

3. The guidance for visitor searches is set out in the National Offender Management Service Framework 3.1 PSI 3.1 and can be accessed at www.justice.gov.uk. The current framework makes specific reference only to babies.

4. https://www.jrf.org.uk/report/poverty-and-disadvantage-among-prisoners-families

*2015*

**www.barnardos.org.uk**

### Mini glossary

**Contraband** – *goods that have been banned or are illegal.*

**Intervention** – *when someone is confronted by their family and friends in order to address a serious issue.*

# Activities

## Brainstorm

1. What is the age of criminal responsibility in the UK?

2. Have crime rates gone up or down in recent years?

## Oral activity

3. Restorative justice involves communication between an offender and their victim with the aim that both can find a way forward and build a more positive future. Role play a situation where one of you is the victim and the other the offender. As the victim you might wish to discuss the impact the crime has had. As the offender you could talk about why you did the crime and offer an apology. What did you learn from this exchange? Do you feel it was effective?

## Research activity

4. Do you think films such as *Ocean's 11* or *Lock, Stock and Two Smoking Barrels* glamourise crime and criminal activity? What about video games such as the *Grand Theft Auto* series? Give reasons for your answer.

## Written activity

5. Write an advice guide for young victims of crime, explaining how they can report a crime and what support they will receive afterwards.

## Moral dilemma

6. "One of the downsides of freedom is you have to have some crime." Discuss this statement as a class.

## Design activities

7. Design a poster or a series of online banners that will raise awareness of knife crime in the UK.

8. Design a website that will give young people information about what to do if they have been the victim of a crime.

# The ten principles of crime prevention

These principles can help you to reduce the chance of crime happening at your home, your place of work or your business. It's not a case of having to use all of the ten principles at once, you may find using just one of them could help you or it may be a combination of several of them (it all depends on your individual circumstances).

The ten principles of crime prevention are:

## Target hardening

This basically refers to making something harder for an offender to access. This could be:

➢ Upgrading the locks on your doors or windows

➢ Replacing doors or windows if they are particularly weak or the frames are in a poor state of repair

➢ Fitting sash jammers to doors or windows

➢ Making sure that sheds or outbuildings are secure.

## Target removal

This principle can be cost free in most cases. It is all about making sure that a potential target for an offender is out of view, so it won't attract their attention in the first place. This could be:

➢ Not leaving items in an unoccupied vehicle

➢ Putting your vehicle in the garage if you have one

➢ Making sure that you don't leave attractive items on view through your kitchen window – i.e. laptops, phones, keys, bags

➢ Not leaving attractive objects such as games consoles, iPads, collectables or antiques on full view in downstairs rooms.

## Removing the means to commit crime

This principle is to make sure that items which might help an offender commit an offence are hidden away. As with target removal, this principle can also be relatively cost free. This could be:

➢ Not leaving garden tools out once you have finished with them

➢ Making sure that ladders are not left out

➢ Keeping wheelie bins out of reach from an offender, as they may climb on them or use them to transport items away from a scene

➢ Making sure that bricks or rubble are cleared up.

## Reducing the pay-off

An offender will want to maximise the amount gained from taking the risk of committing an offence and there are ways to reduce their potential pay-off. This could be:

➢ Security marking your property

➢ The use of a domestic safe to secure valuable or sentimental items

➢ Using dummy/fake stock in shop windows

➢ Making sure that you don't leave vehicle keys in an obvious place.

## Access control

This principle suggests looking at measures that will control access to a location, a person or an objective. This could be:

➢ Locking your doors and windows and removing the keys from the lock once you have done it

➢ Making sure that car doors are locked and that sunroofs and windows are shut

➢ Check that fencing, hedges, walls and other boundary treatments are in a good state of repair and provide no access points

➢ Putting a security system in place at a commercial site – i.e. entrance/exit barriers, a security guard, ID Card systems.

## Surveillance

Offenders obviously do not want to be seen and look for ways to hide to help them commit their crimes. Improving surveillance around homes, businesses or public places is very important. This could be:

➢ Not having an 8ft high hedge in front of your home that simply provides a barrier for an offender to work unseen behind

➢ Adding CCTV to a commercial site or public place

➢ Having a Neighbourhood Watch Scheme in your street

➢ Encouraging neighbours or employees to be more alert in their day to day business – i.e. whilst walking the dog or taking their lunch break around places of work.

# Environmental change

Offenders like familiarity with an area, they like knowing routes in and out of an area and knowing that they can leave with ease if required. Environments should also not look like they have been forgotten about and that no one cares. This could be:

➤ Working with the police and local authority to close a footpath

➤ Making sure that graffiti and domestic/commercial waste is cleared up

➤ Reporting issues with fly-tipping or broken street lights to the relevant authority

➤ Organising or taking part in environmental action days.

# Rule setting

Putting rules in place to make a place more secure. This may require a change in our habits. This could be:

➤ Introduce a new rule in your home that the last person leaving or entering the property should lock the door and remove the keys

➤ Informing visitors to commercial sites that they must report to reception on arrival

➤ Making sure employees wear ID cards at all times

➤ Informing users that a particular site is closed between certain times and should not be accessed during these times.

# Increasing the chances of being caught

As previously mentioned, offenders do not want to be seen and they look for places around the site to hide when they are looking to commit an offence. There are ways that we can increase the chances of an offender being seen. This could be:

➤ Making sure that domestic security lighting is in place and in working order

➤ The use of good quality CCTV, especially on commercial sites and around public places

➤ Reducing the height of hedges to the front of properties and making sure overgrown shrubbery doesn't provide places for offenders to hide

➤ Improving boundary protection or upgrading security to delay an offender, meaning they would have to spend more time in/at a location.

# Deflecting offenders

Deterring an offender or deflecting their intentions can be done in a number of ways. Some approaches will be done in partnership with specific agencies/organisations. Others can be done around the home. This could be:

➤ The use of timer switches to make our homes look occupied if they are empty after the hours of darkness

➤ Running youth diversionary schemes with partner agencies

➤ Referring offenders to drug rehabilitation programmes

➤ Taking every opportunity to implement crime prevention measures around homes and businesses.

When you are looking at using the principles of crime prevention to improve security around your home or business, the best way to approach it is to look at your home or premises as if you were the offender. Identify the weak spots, vulnerable points and hidden areas and prioritise these as areas for improvement. Contact our Crime Prevention Officers before you undertake any improvements and they will work with you to ensure that you are taking the best approach possible for your respective circumstances.

**www.westyorkshire.police.uk**

# Forecasting the time and place of crime hotspots

University College London (UCL) researchers worked directly with police forces to launch the use of crime mapping and forecasting methods to prevent crime. In areas where they carried this out crimes such as burglary fell by 20–66%.

Over 35,000 cases of burglary are reported across England and Wales each month. Predicting where and when offences will occur has until recently proven very difficult. Combined with the incorrect belief that preventing crime in one location simply moves all of it elsewhere, this has led to a traditional police emphasis on detection. While detections are certainly important, as Benjamin Franklin noted, an ounce of prevention is worth a pound of cure.

Over the last decade, Researchers at UCL Security and Crime Science have developed tools that forecast the time and place at which crime is committed more accurately than was previously possible, and provides training in the use of these tools. Starting with the observation that crime hotspots are slippery, with many moving around over time, Professors Shane Johnson, Kate Bowers and Ken Pease demonstrated that the risk of burglary shows a pattern similar to a contagious disease. Better prediction enables police officers to develop tactics that locate officers in the right place at the right time to prevent a crime from occurring.

Their research suggests that forecasting is possible because offenders often adopt 'foraging' strategies. They maximise benefits whilst reducing risk, for example by returning to houses they have already burgled, or to similar houses in the neighbourhood, for a matter of days or weeks, until they have exhausted the best opportunities or they begin to worry about detection by "going to the well once too often". Targeting crime prevention activity or police patrols in very small areas where a burglary has recently occurred can reduce the total number of burglaries.

Training provided for, and engagement with, practitioners such as the police (by Professors Bowers, Johnson and Pease and Spencer Chainey), has led to the implementation of successful crime prevention strategies based on this approach. In 2010, Greater Manchester Police in Trafford (population 226,578) reduced burglary by using predictive maps to send police patrols and other resources to those areas expected to be most at risk. There was a 38% reduction in burglary over two years and the approach was extended to other crimes, achieving, for example, a 29% reduction in theft from motor vehicles.

"It was an enormous but worthwhile effort to move this from the page to the reality of an operational setting. I'm very proud we developed a successful means for the mapping of future risk of crime, accompanied with a complementary system of police deployment. This was subsequently successfully adopted by a significant number of UK police forces." – Inspector Vincent Jones, Greater Manchester Police

Similar successes have been seen elsewhere in the country. In 2012 in North West Leeds (population 321,000), which had previously experienced the highest burglary rate in the country, a 48% decrease in burglary was accompanied by increased public confidence in the police. Similar approaches were used in Kent, West Mercia and London. In Canada, a Neighbourhood Empowerment Team in the city of Edmonton developed an intervention based on the research, which reduced burglary by 66% in the trial area.

This has fed into policy at every level; researchers have served as expert witnesses to parliamentary select committees, advised Her Majesty's Inspectorate of Constabularies, and contributed to training courses provided by the College of Policing. The work has also received extensive media coverage through the BBC and the *New Scientist*.

*16 December 2014*

# The death penalty

Every day, people are executed by the state as punishment for a variety of crimes – sometimes for acts that should not be criminalised. In some countries it can be for who you sleep with, in others it is reserved for acts of terror and murder.

Some countries execute people who were under 18 years old when the crime was committed, others use the death penalty against people who suffer mental problems. Before people die they are often imprisoned for years on 'death row'. Not knowing when their time is up, or whether they will see their families one last time.

The death penalty is cruel, inhumane and degrading. Amnesty opposes the death penalty at all times – regardless of who is accused, the crime, guilt or innocence or method of execution.

We have been working to end executions since 1977, when only 16 countries had abolished the death penalty in law or practice. Today, the number has risen to 140 – nearly two-thirds of countries around the world.

We know that, together, we can end the death penalty everywhere. Hafez Ibrahim was about to be executed in Yemen in 2007 when he sent a mobile text message to Amnesty. It was a message that saved his life. "I owe my life to Amnesty. Now I dedicate that life to campaigning against the death penalty."

## The problem
### Why the death penalty is wrong

**Denial of human rights.** Sentencing someone to death denies them the right to life – something which is protected in the Universal Declaration of Human Rights.

**Irreversible, and mistakes happen.** Execution is the ultimate, final punishment: the risk of executing an innocent person can never be eliminated. Since 1973, for example, 150 US prisoners sent to death row have later been declared not guilty. Others have been executed despite serious doubts about their guilt.

**Does not discourage crime.** Countries who execute commonly cite the death penalty as a way to put people off from committing crime. There is no evidence that the death penalty is any more effective in reducing crime than imprisonment.

The death penalty is a symptom of a culture of violence, not a solution to it.

**Often used within 'unfair' justice systems.** Some of the countries executing the most people have deeply unfair legal systems. The 'top' three executing countries – China, Iran and Iraq – have issued death sentences after unfair trials. Many death sentences are issued after 'confessions' that have been obtained through torture.

**Discriminatory.** You are more likely to be sentenced to death if you are poor or belong to a racial, ethnic or religious minority because of discrimination in the justice system. Also, poor groups have less access to the legal resources needed to defend themselves.

Used as a political tool. The authorities in some countries, for example Iran and Sudan, use the death penalty to punish political opponents.

## Amnesty is calling for:

➢ Countries who still use the death penalty to immediately stop all executions.
➢ Countries who have already stopped executing people, need to take this punishment off their legal books for all crimes, permanently.
➢ All death sentences should be commuted to prison sentences.

## Execution methods

There are many and varied types of execution used around the world today, including:

➢ Beheading
➢ Electrocution
➢ Hanging
➢ Lethal injection
➢ Shooting in the back of the head and by firing squad.

The above information, which has been slightly edited, is reprinted with kind permission from Amnesty International. Please visit www.amnesty.org.uk for further information and to read their annual review of the death penalty worldwide.
© Amnesty International 2016

www.amnesty.org.uk

# Support for the death penalty falls below 50% for first time

Findings from NatCen's British Social Attitudes today reveal that fewer than half of people in Britain back the death penalty – the first time support has dropped below 50% since NatCen began asking the public its view on capital punishment in 1986.

NatCen's annual survey of the public's view on political and social issues shows only 48% of people now back the death penalty for "some crimes", down from 54% in 2013.

Support for the death penalty stood at 74% in 1986, and then fell during the 1990s to 59% by 1998. The previous low of 52% was recorded in 2001.

Young people are consistently less likely to agree with the death penalty as older people. However, the difference is not that marked: 43% of 18–24s compared with 52% of those aged 65+ agree with the death penalty for some crimes. We also find big political differences on the issue, with UKIP voters far more likely to support the death penalty than the public as a whole (75% compared with 48%).

Rachel Ormston, Co-Head of Social Attitudes at NatCen Social Research said: "The big change in public attitudes to the death penalty came in the 1990s

at a time when attitudes to a range of other issues, like same-sex relationships and sex before marriage were also liberalising. This more recent change is interesting because attitudes have stayed fairly steady for a number of years. It could be the continuation of this liberalising trend or, perhaps, a response to the shocking botched executions in the United States that were widely reported in April and July of last year."

## Notes

*British Social Attitudes: the 32nd Report* was published on 26 March 2015 and is freely available at: www.bsa. natcen.ac.uk.

Sample and approach – The 2014 survey consisted of 2,878 interviews with a representative, random sample of adults in Britain. Interviewing was mainly carried out between August and October 2014, with a small number of interviews taking place in November 2014. 2,376 people were asked about their views on the death penalty.

*26 March 2015*

**www.bsa.natcen.ac.uk**

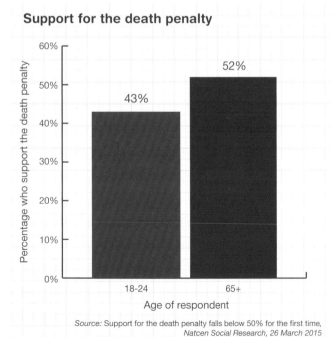

**Support for the death penalty**

Source: Support for the death penalty falls below 50% for the first time, Natcen Social Research, 26 March 2015

# FactCheck: are police cuts putting the public at risk?

*By Patrick Worrall*

## The claim

*"There can be no doubt that the drastic cuts in force budgets is doing real harm to the ability of the service to protect the public."* – Steve White, chairman, Police Federation of England and Wales, 29 January 2015.

## The background

Police officer numbers in England and Wales have fallen to their lowest levels since 2001, according to the latest official statistics.

The Police Federation – the closest thing bobbies have to a union – is outraged, while others note that crime rates have fallen even as forces wrestle with budget cuts.

Just how thinly stretched are the police these days? And should we be worried?

## The analysis

The latest Home Office estimates of police strength in England and Wales are for September last year.

The overall police workforce (including officers, Police Community Support Officers and staff) dropped from just under 245,000 in March 2010 to just under 208,000 in September 2014.

That's a loss of more than 36,000 police personnel or, as the Police Federation says, that's equal to losing nine of the smaller police forces at their 2010 strength. It's like going from 43 constabularies in England and Wales to 34.

Forces have cut police staff more than officers, but officer strength has also fallen considerably – from 143,734 to 127,075 or by 11.6 per cent since March 2010.

Force cuts vary a lot from region to region. The following table shows the Police Federation breakdown for cuts to the top and bottom three forces:

| Force | 2010 (March) | 2014 (September) | % reduction since 2010 |
|---|---|---|---|
| Cleveland | 1724.42 | 1342.52 | 22.15% |
| Staffordshire | 2161.05 | 1683.76 | 22.09% |
| Humberside | 2057.62 | 1640.75 | 20.26% |
| Norfolk | 1662.18 | 1569.81 | 5.56% |
| North Yorkshire | 1485.67 | 1403.5 | 5.53% |
| Metropolitan Police | 33366.55 | 31583.05 | 5.35% |

Some forces have seen officer numbers drop by more than 20 per cent.

Britain's biggest force, the Metropolitan Police, has managed to protect officer numbers from the cuts to a certain extent, although there are still fewer than the 32,000 or so officers promised by the mayor of London, Boris Johnson, while he was running for election.

## Bobbies on the beat

While there is no dispute that police officer numbers are down, Her Majesty's Inspectorate of Constabulary reckons forces have managed to shift a bigger proportion of them into frontline roles.

The police watchdog estimates that 93 per cent of officers left after the cuts will be deployed on the front line, rising from 89 per cent in 2010.

According to the House of Commons Library, the overall effect is that frontline officer numbers have still been falling overall, but less sharply.

This suggests that forces have taken steps to minimise the effect of the cuts on the public, although these figures of course relate to the number of officers on the payroll, not the number available at any given time.

## If you need a bobby right now, how many will be available?

The Police Fed has given Channel 4 News an interesting snapshot of how many officers were actually on duty in 11 forces across England and Wales at a random time – 11am yesterday [2 February 2015].

The Fed's numbers include uniformed personnel only, not detectives. They only count people who are actually on duty, not training and so on.

There is a huge variation in how many officers are available compared to the size of the local population.

At 11am on Monday, there were 4,136 uniformed officers on duty in the Met Police area. That's about one police officer for every 1,740 residents.

In Greater Manchester there were 398 officers on call – or one officer covering 6,281 Mancunians.

And in Kent there were only 203 officers on shift covering a population of 1.7 million, or one officer between 8,374 people.

This is only a snapshot, and we don't have historic figures to compare it with, so we don't know whether officers are generally more thinly spread than they were in 2010.

## Does it matter?

The Association of Chief Police Officers noted that crime rates have been falling throughout this time of reduced spending, saying: "Our effectiveness can't be solely measured on police numbers. It is the service we deliver that matters to the public."

Has crime really fallen? That is what police figures say, but there is a growing chorus of doubt about the numbers recorded by forces.

Nevertheless, figures from the Crime Survey for England and Wales, collected independently from the police, agree crime has been falling in England and Wales over the last ten years or so, as it has in a number of other western countries.

And independent data from health services appears to show that violence is on the decline in England and Wales. Again, this is in line with trends in a number of other countries.

It may seem strange that crime should fall as police dwindles, but there is actually little agreement among the experts about what drives long-term changes in crime rates.

Criminologist Ben Bradford reviewed the available evidence in 2011 and concluded: "It is too early to say... that there is a direct causal link between higher numbers of police and lower crime."

Some studies have found a link between higher police numbers and falls in property crime, but establishing cause and effect is a difficult task.

## The verdict

There is little dispute about the scale of the cuts dished out to police forces since 2010. The total police workforce in England and Wales has fallen by about 15 per cent and the number of officers has been cut by more than 11 per cent.

But there is some evidence that forces have risen to the challenge by putting more officers in frontline roles.

The Police Federation's snapshot of police officers on call yesterday is an insight into how thinly stretched some forces are – but we don't know whether the ratio of available officers to members of the public is getting better or worse.

The government may well take some comfort from the fact that crime, on all the evidence, is falling.

Rather than debating any of this, the Police Federation says crime rates are only part of the story.

Chairman Steve White said: "We hear that crime is falling but this only measures a snapshot of police activity.

"What we do not hear about is the extreme pressure these government cuts are placing on officers' ability to prevent terrorist attacks, manage sex offenders in the community, protect children from sexual exploitation and return missing persons to their families among other key issues."

*3 February 2015*

**blogs.channel4.com/factcheck**

# Armed police to increase by "up to 50 per cent"

Exclusive: Theresa May, the Home Secretary, told forces to expand firearms teams so they can "quickly and forcefully" respond to Paris-style attacks.

*By David Barrett, Home Affairs Correspondent*

Theresa May, the Home Secretary, has asked police forces to increase the number of firearms officers by up to 50 per cent so they can respond "quickly and forcefully" to a Paris-style terror attack, *The Telegraph* can disclose.

Mrs May wrote to chief constables and police and crime commissioners soon after the attacks, which killed 130, asking them to upgrade their firearms capabilities.

A national review is now underway to establish which shire county forces – and metropolitan forces outside London – should receive the lion's share of funds earmarked for extra armed officers in last November's comprehensive spending review.

The Metropolitan Police, Britain's largest police force, confirmed its number of firearms-carrying officers will be boosted by 600 to 2,800, amid the threat of "marauding" terrorist gunmen striking in the capital.

Mrs May's letter, sent just 12 days after Paris, confirmed that money secured from the Treasury would be used for a "major uplift in firearms capability and capacity so we can respond quickly and forcefully to firearms attacks".

Firearms response teams would be increased by "up to 50 per cent" and numbers of tactically-trained counter-terrorism armed officers would also increase, she said.

As the Met became the first force to announce a boost in numbers Sir Bernard Hogan-Howe, the Commissioner,

said: "I have decided that we take the steps to increase these numbers on a permanent basis.

"This increase will more than double the number of armed response vehicles on our streets and grow a highly trained specialist part of our capability.

"This is because we know that the threat we currently face is likely to be a spontaneous attack that requires a fast response to deal with it."

He added that it was an "expensive option" but was "vital to keeping us safe".

The National Police Chiefs Council (NPCC) is leading work on potential threats in the regions which merit additional firearms cover.

Deputy Chief Constable Simon Chesterman, who leads on armed policing for the NPCC, told *The Telegraph*: "We are working on a significant national uplift to be allocated to forces where the threat is assessed to be greatest."

However, chief constables are also understood to be drawing up additional plans to train extra armed officers from within existing budgets.

A spokesman for Kent police and crime commissioner said: "The Home Secretary has indicated she wants forces to increase their capability by up to 50 per cent.

"That request was sent to us on November 25.

"Kent currently has 74 armed officers so we are preparing plans for an additional 37 to fulfil that request.

"We are aiming to recruit an additional 24 firearms officers initially. This is in train already."

Anthony Stansfeld, police and crime commissioner for Thames Valley Police, said: "We are doing a study to see how we can lift the number of firearms officers.

"We shall have to buy some more guns, by the sounds of it.

"We are cognisant of the fact we have to take some action."

It came as a former police chief said she believed Britain's regional forces would not be capable of responding in depth to a terrorism attack similar to the events that unfolded in Paris last year.

Ex-Northumbria chief constable Sue Sim said it would be "extremely difficult" to find enough armed officers to deal with a large-scale attack spanning multiple sites.

She told 5 Live Daily: "A local force like Northumbria could not, in any way, cope with that type of incident other

## DID YOU KNOW?

*Police officers in Great Britain (England, Scotland and Wales) do not carry firearms, except in special circumstances. However, in Northern Ireland all police officers do carry firearms.*

*Although the Met want to bring the total number of armed offices in London to 2,800, overall 92% of the Met offices will still remain unarmed.*

*Source: Met Police to get 600 more armed police to boost terror response, BBC, 14 January 2016.*

than giving a very, very initial first response, and I would suggest that would be the same for any of the forces in the country."

Before the Paris atrocities Mrs May indicated that police forces could be stripped of their own firearms teams, and forced to share them with neighbouring forces.

In the November attacks in the French capital three Isil gunmen armed with automatic rifles spent 2 hours and 40 minutes inside the Bataclan theatre, firing into the tightly-packed audience of 1,500 before beginning a siege which ended when anti-terrorist police stormed the building.

Two of the gunmen blew themselves up with suicide vests, while the third was shot dead by police.

Earlier the terrorists had targeted a number of pavement cafes.

Among those killed was Nick Alexander, 36, from Colchester, Essex, who worked for the band Eagles of Death Metal selling merchandise.

*14 January 2016*

**www.telegraph.co.uk**

## Mini glossary

***Cognisant*** – *to be aware of.*

# Decriminalising drugs

Is decriminalising all drugs the way to reduce drug crime and end the war on drugs for good?

*By Christina Hughes*

Drug-related crimes take up a lot of police time and clog up the court and justice system. This time could be used to free up resources and tackle crimes that are even more serious. Some people also feel that the punishment for possession of certain drugs, such as marijuana, is too harsh; it can ruin lives for what, they argue, is a minor offence. Decriminalising drugs would help to solve these problems.

## What is the difference between decriminalising drugs and legalising drugs?

Legalising all drugs would mean that producing, selling and possessing would be completely within the law. If drugs were decriminalised, however, the production, sale and possession of drugs would remain illegal, but would no longer be classed as criminal offences. This would mean that, instead of jail time, people would be issued a warning or a fine.

## Potential positive outcomes

By decriminalising drugs:

➢ Big criminal empires would lose their power and control of the drug market.

➢ People would stop getting in trouble for possession of small amounts of drugs.

➢ The police force could redirect their focus onto other serious crimes.

➢ Rather than treating addicts like criminals, they would be treated more like patients who need help. This in turn would mean that people would be more likely to come forward and seek treatment for drug addiction.

## Concerns

There is a concern that by decriminalising drugs more people would begin using them. It may also encourage people to use harder drugs.

## Case study: Portugal

In 2001, the Portuguese government decriminalised the use of all drugs. This included everything from marijuana to heroin. Drugs are still illegal in Portugal, with drug dealers and traffickers still being sent to jail, but today Portuguese authorities don't arrest anyone found holding what's considered less than a 10-day supply of an illicit drug: a gram of heroin, ecstasy or amphetamine; two grams of cocaine; or 25 grams of cannabis.

Rather than treating possession and use of small quantities of drugs as a criminal issue, Portugal looks at it as a public health issue; drug offenders receive a written warning and are ordered to appear before so- called "dissuasion panels" made up of legal, social and psychological experts. People who repeatedly come before the panels may be prescribed treatment, ranging from motivational counselling to opiate substitution therapy.

## Interesting facts

After drugs were decriminalised, Portugal saw:

➢ An initial increase of drug use but then a decline.

➢ Drug use among those most at risk of starting, 15- to 24-year-olds, has seen an overall decline.

➢ Drug-induced deaths have decreased steeply.

➢ HIV infection rates among injecting drug users have been reduced at a steady pace.

## Sources

*Why hardly anyone dies from a drug overdose in Portugal*
https://www.washingtonpost.com/news/wonk/wp/2015/06/05/why-hardly-anyone-dies-from-a-drug-overdose-in-portugal/

*Portugal's Example: what happened after it decriminalised all drugs, from weed to heroin*
https://news.vice.com/article/ungass-portugal-what-happened-after-decriminalization-drugs-weed-to-heroin

*14 years after decriminalising all drugs, here's what Portugal looks like*
http://mic.com/articles/110344/14-years-after-portugal-decriminalized-all-drugs-here-s-what-s-happening#.9CSJ5i4Gv

*Drug decriminalisation in Portugal: setting the record straight*
http://www.tdpf.org.uk/resources/publications/drug-decriminalisation-portugal-setting-record-straight

*12 May 2016*

*The above article is written by Christina Hughes on behalf of Independence Educational Publishers.*
*© Christina Hughes/Independence Educational Publishers 2016*

# Activities

## Brainstorm

1. What are the ten principles of crime prevention?

## Oral activity

2. "All police officers should carry firearms in Great Britain." Discuss this statement in small groups and feedback to the class.

## Research activities

3. Research the law on carrying guns in the UK, the USA and one other country of your choice. Summarise your findings and include some details about the rate of gun-related crime in each country. You could also include graphs.

4. Choose a country where the death penalty is still in use and research Amnesty International's work in that country. Why does Amnesty International believe the death penalty should be banned? Write some notes and share with a classmate.

## Written activities

5. "Some crimes are so horrific, the death penalty is the only appropriate punishment. The victim's loved ones deserve that." "The main problem with the death penalty is we can never be 100% sure of someone's guilt. That is why it should never be reintroduced." Do you agree with either of these views? What other arguments might be put forward for and against the death penalty? Write a summary of the arguments for and against, and give your own conclusion.

6. Read *Forecasting the time and place of crime hotspots* on page 18. Write a summary of the article and explain what a crime hotspot is and how it would be possible to 'forecast' them.

## Moral dilemma

7. "Social media has driven an increase in hate crime and should be banned." Debate this statement as a class, with half of you arguing in agreement and half of you against it.

## Design activity

8. Design an app that could be used to help prevent crime.

# Key facts

- Offences involving knives and sharp instruments increased by 2% in the year ending March 2015. (page 1)

- It is illegal to: sell a knife of any kind to anyone under 18 years old (16- to 18-year-olds in Scotland can buy cutlery and kitchen knives). (page 4)

- The maximum penalty for an adult carrying a knife is four years in prison and a fine of £5,000. (page 4)

- Approximately one-third of 11–17-year-olds report experiencing physical violence within the last year. One-quarter of 11–24-year-olds say they experienced some form of abuse or neglect during childhood. (page 5)

- Existing vulnerabilities, such as a long-standing illness or disability, appear to really increase children and young people's vulnerability to crime. (page 5)

- Only 13% of violent offences and 15% of thefts are reported by young victims. Similarly, only 5–13% of adults who were victims of childhood sexual abuse reported it at the time. (page 5)

- On 23 October 2015, the prison population in England and Wales was 85,106. (page 9)

- Prison has a poor record for reducing reoffending – 45% of adults are reconvicted within one year of release. (page 9)

- Prison sentences are getting longer. The average prison sentence is now nearly more than four months longer than 20 years ago ay 15.9 months. (page 9)

- At the end of March 2015 there were 1,004 children in custody in England and Wales. 44 children were aged 14 or younger. (page 9)

- It is estimated that more than 17,240 children were separated from their mother in 2010 by imprisonment. (page 10)

- The Government estimates that about 200,000 children are affected by parental imprisonment each year in England and Wales, and each week, children make nearly 10,000 visits to public prisons. (page 13)

- UCL researchers worked directly with police forces to launch the use of crime mapping and forecasting methods to prevent crime. In areas where they carried this out crimes such as burglary fell by 20–66%. (page 18)

- Over 35,000 cases of burglary are reported across England and Wales each month. (page 18)

- Today, nearly two-thirds of countries around the world (140 countries) have abolished the death penalty in law or practice. (page 19)

- Since 1973, 150 US prisoners sent to death row have later been declared not guilty. (page 19)

- The overall police workforce (including officers, Police Community Support Officers and staff) dropped from just under 245,000 in March 2010 to just under 208,000 in September 2014. (page 20)

# Glossary

**Age of criminal responsibility** – The minimum age of criminal responsibility in England and Wales was set at ten in the 1963 Children and Young Person's Act. In the 1998 Crime and Disorder Act, Labour abolished the principle of doli incapax, whereby the prosecution had to prove that a child under 14 appearing in the criminal court knew and fully understood what he or she was doing was seriously wrong.

**Crime** – Crime may be defined as an act or omission prohibited or punished by law. A 'criminal offence' includes any infringement of the criminal law, from homicide to riding a bicycle without lights. What is classified as a crime is supposed to reflect the values of society and to reinforce those values. If an act is regarded as harmful to society or its citizens, it is often, but not always, classified as a criminal offence.

**Custody** – In criminal terminology, being 'in custody' refers to someone being held in spite of their wishes, either by the police while awaiting trial (remanded in custody), or, having received a custodial sentence, in prison or other secure accommodation. If someone has spent time on remand, that time is taken off their prison sentence.

**Deterrent** – Any threat or punishment which is seen to deter someone from a certain action: the threat of prison, for example, is expected to function as a deterrent to criminal behaviour.

**Non-custodial sentence** – A punishment which does not require someone convicted of a crime to be held in prison or another closed institution. Community sentences, restraining orders and fines are all types of non-custodial punishment.

**Peer/youth court** – An alternative approach to sentencing for young people. In the peer/youth court system, a young person who is charged with a crime appears in front of a jury of their peers for sentencing. The person being charged must agree to take part in the process.

**Rehabilitation** – The process by which an offender can learn, through therapy and education, to be a useful member of society on completing their sentence.

**Reoffending rate** – The rate at which offenders, having been convicted of a crime and punished, will then go on to commit another crime (implying that the punishment was ineffectual as a crime deterrent).

**Restorative justice** – This usually involves communication between an offender and their victim, family members, and possibly other people from the community or people affected by the crime. The purpose of the communication is to discuss the offending behaviour and come up with ways for the person to 'repay' the victim or community for their crime.

**Sentence** – The punishment given by a judge to a convicted offender at the end of a criminal trial. This generally takes the form of a fine, a community punishment, a discharge or a period of imprisonment.